The KING Who Barked

Real Animals Who Ruled

BY **CHARLOTTE FOLTZ JONES**

ILLUSTRATED BY **YAYO**

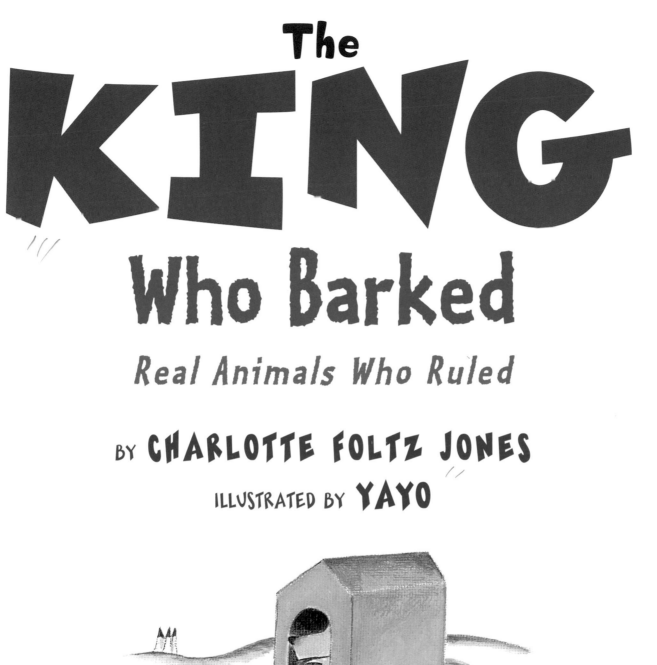

Holiday House / New York

gift 7-3-10 $16.95

Library of Congress Cataloging-in-Publication Data
Jones, Charlotte Foltz.
The king who barked : real animals who ruled / by Charlotte Foltz Jones ; illustrated by Yayo. — 1st ed.
p. cm.
Includes bibliographical references and index.
ISBN 978-0-8234-1925-8 (hardcover)
1. Famous animals—Anecdotes—Juvenile literature.
2. Famous animals—Folklore—Juvenile literature.
3. Human-animal relationships—History—Juvenile literature.
I. Yayo. II. Title.
QL793.J66 2009
636—dc22
2008025669

To the street dogs of Mesitas — Yayo

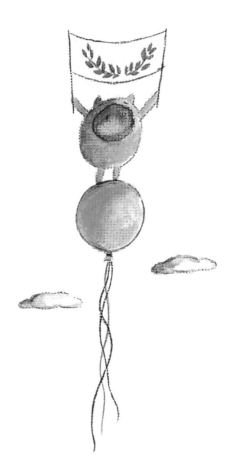

CONTENTS

INTRODUCTION

Can it be true? Really, really true? Is it possible that an animal could hold an important office? Be a king? A mayor? A councilman—er, rather, a council-rhinoceros?

Is it true? These incidents are recorded in books, journals, magazines, and newspapers. We presume they are true.

But it's important to remember that many of the incidents in this book from a thousand or two thousand years ago were stories, legends, and histories that were repeated around fires or at gatherings. When the stories were finally written down, many years might have passed since the actual events.

Modern-day elected animal-officials, such as the goat-mayor in Lajitas, Texas, are probably figureheads or symbols. The people who live in those towns are intelligent and have governments that work well without actually relying on a goat-mayor. So the goat serves as a pretty-faced symbol of leadership.

This book is intended to bring joy and humor to the reader, as well as to stretch the imagination. What if an animal was *really* in charge of making decisions in your town?

AFRICA
Dogs Rule: *Ethiopia's Dog-King*

COUNTRY: Ethiopia
YEAR: around 60 CE

Somewhere near the Nile River in Africa two thousand years ago, a very strange thing happened. A dog became a king!

Pliny the Elder (c. 23–79 CE), a Roman statesman and author, wrote that the Tonobari and Ptoenphae people in Ethiopia had chosen a dog for their king.

The dog-king lived in a palace and had his own personal attendants, officers, and guards. He commanded his people through his actions: If he scratched himself, he was not angry; if he barked, he was. If he wagged his tail, he was pleased. If he licked a man's hand, he was honoring that man. But if the dog-king growled, he was displeased; and the man he growled at might be sentenced to captivity or even death.

Sadly, Pliny the Elder didn't write down the dog's name. Maybe he couldn't spell it.

EUROPE

Horse Sense: *Incitatus*

COUNTRY: Roman Empire   **YEAR:** around 40 CE

Two thousand years ago, Emperor Caligula ruled the Roman Empire. Caligula was not an ordinary ruler. He did some odd things: He declared that he was a god. He renamed the month of September "Germanicus" after himself. (Germanicus was his real name.) He ordered the heads removed from Rome's sculptures and replaced them with models of his own head.

Caligula, however, loved his horses, and he loved horse racing. Incitatus was his favorite horse. The night before a race, Caligula's soldiers stood guard around Incitatus's stable to keep everything very quiet. Caligula wanted to ensure that Incitatus's sleep would not be disturbed.

Caligula was so fond of his horse that he had a marble stable built with a manger made of ivory. Eighteen servants attended to the horse. Incitatus wore a jeweled collar and a purple blanket. He was fed oats mixed with flakes of gold. The horse even had a house where human guests stayed when they came to dine. The house, of course, was staffed by servants for both the visiting dignitaries and the horse. Caligula declared that Incitatus was to be made a consul (a member of his government). And it would have happened; but Caligula was killed in 41 CE, before the appointment was actually made.

You Dirty Dog: *King Henry I's Dog*

COUNTRY: Germany   **YEAR:** 933 CE

Henry I of Germany was also known as Henry the Fowler. Legend says he got the name because he was out hunting fowl when a messenger arrived to tell him he had been named king. King Henry I had his hands full trying to defend his country against the attacks of the Magyars. In about 924 CE, he got a lucky break: He captured a high-ranking Magyar leader.

King Henry agreed to release the prisoner in exchange for a nine-year truce. The Magyars said they would agree to the truce *if* Henry also paid an annual tribute (a kind of tax). King Henry agreed.

Once the truce began, King Henry I didn't just sit around watching the grass grow. He built fortifications and castles. He also trained "warrior farmers" to fight on horseback.

In 933, Henry felt certain his army could defeat the Magyars, so he stopped paying the tribute money, which made the Magyars mad. On March 15, 933, the fighting began near Meresburg, Germany. King Henry I prevailed in the battle. When the Magyars surrendered, legend says King Henry I sent a mangy, dirty dog with no ears and no tail to govern the Magyar people. King Henry I insisted they pay homage to the dog.

One legend states that the dog's name was Hungari and the people who paid him homage became known as Hungarians. However, historians claim that this is strictly a myth.

It's a Dog's Life: *King Saur*

COUNTRY: Norway   YEAR: early 1100s

In the early twelfth century, during the days of the Vikings, no one in Norway's Uplands liked King Eystein. Behind his back, the people of Trondheim called him King Eystein the Evil or Eystein the Bad. The king wasn't dumb. Eystein the Bad knew the people didn't like him. So he made his son, Onund, their king. But the people didn't like Onund any better, and they soon got rid of him.

Eystein the Bad was furious. He said something like, "So you did not like me for your king, and you did not like my son for your king. Okay, folks, make your choice: You can have Thorir Faxi, my thrall [who was his manservant and also known as Thorir the Hairy], or you can have my dog Saur as your king."

When the voting was finished, it was unanimous. Since Saur, the dog, would give the people more independence, they elected the dog as their king. A high throne was prepared for King Saur I, and a gold and silver collar and chain were made for him. Courtiers were appointed to serve King Saur I. When the weather was bad, they carried the dog on their shoulders so he wouldn't get his feet wet. The king signed decrees with his paw. The people believed Saur had the wisdom of three men, and it was said he spoke one word for every two that he barked. King Saur I reigned for three years, but his reign ended in tragedy. One day wolves attacked the royal sheep. King Saur I went to the sheep's defense and attacked, but the powerful wolves prevailed. The king died in battle, ending the reign of King Saur I, the dog-king of Norway.

ASIA

Puppy Love: *Emperor Ling Ti's Pekingese Dogs*

COUNTRY: China   **YEAR:** 168–189 CE

As long ago as three thousand years, the emperors of China adored their Pekingese dogs. They loved them so much that they assigned them ranks. Some were dukes; others were princes. Special servants were appointed to care for the dogs. The dogs were even granted royal revenues (money)!

Emperor Ling Ti, ruler of the Han dynasty from 168 to 189 CE, had four Pekingese "bodyguards." Two of them preceded him into the royal court, holding their tails high and barking. The other two followed behind, carrying the hem of his robe in their mouths.

The emperor gave some of his dogs the rank of *k'ai fu*, which would be comparable to a viceroy. To others he gave the rank of *yi tung*, or imperial guardian. Soldiers guarded these royal dogs; chefs prepared the best meat and rice for them.

Emperor Ling Ti had one favorite dog, which was given an official Chin Hsien hat and belt. The hat must have seemed enormous when placed on the small dog, since it was eight inches high and ten inches from front to back. The Chin Hsien was a literary honor, similar to today's Nobel Prize in Literature. Usually only educated scholars received this tribute. Understandably, some government officials serving under Emperor Ling Ti grumbled when the dog received such an important literary award. The dog could neither read nor write!

The Cat's Meow: *Myobu No Omoto*

COUNTRY: Japan   **YEAR:** around 1000 CE

It is said that Japan had only wild cats until the tenth century. When domestic cats from China were introduced, only the emperor and a few noblemen could afford them. They were called *Kara neko*, which means "Chinese cats." Emperor Ichijō, who ruled Japan from 986 to 1011 CE, liked the cats a *lot*.

We can only imagine how happy he was when a mother cat had five kittens at the Imperial Palace in Kyoto! The day was so important that a Japanese author recorded the date: the nineteenth day of the ninth month of the year 999.

The emperor appointed special royal attendants to feed the kittens. The cats were dressed in clothes. One of the cats was so special that Emperor Ichijō made her the fifth lady of the court. Her name, Myobu No Omoto, means "lady-in-waiting." One would think that Myobu No Omoto would be honored by such an important title, but she was probably too busy sleeping to be concerned!

A story is told that one day a dog chased Myobu No Omoto. The cat was rescued unharmed; but she was, after all, a lady of the court. Emperor Ichijō became furious and ordered the dog exiled. He sent the dog's owner to prison.

Day of the Jackal: *A Hero of India*

COUNTRY: India—Golconda   YEAR: 1687

Jackals are doglike outcasts that are native to India. They are scavengers and often eat garbage. No one ever guessed a jackal would be given a title of honor. But that's what happened.

In 1687, two groups were struggling for power in southeastern India near the Bay of Bengal. The Mughals, led by Emperor Aurangzeb, were determined to conquer King Abul Hasan and the Marathas who were defending themselves in a small fortified compound called Golconda.

Late during the night of May 16, 1687, the Mughals launched a sneak attack. Two men quietly climbed ladders up the fort's wall. They were almost at the top when they startled a jackal that was searching for food. The jackal began barking and awakened the Marathas. They rushed to the wall, knocked down the Mughals' ladders, and defended the compound.

The jackal became a hero! Abul Hasan gave the animal a golden collar set with jewels and an ornamental chain, and covered him with a brocade cloth. He gave him a title, *sehtabqa*, which means "friend with three degrees."

Emperor Aurangzeb defeated the Marathas and conquered Golconda on September 21, 1687; but for a brief time, a jackal held a place of high esteem in northern India.

White Elephant: *The Elephants of the Siamese Court*

COUNTRY: Siam (now Thailand)   YEAR: 1854

For centuries the rare white elephant has been revered in Asia. The center of the flag of ancient Siam was adorned with the image of a white elephant.

Three hundred years ago, the king of Siam would not ride on a white elephant because he considered the animal to be as great a lord as himself. White elephants wore crowns, and were rubbed with precious oils and draped in fine ceremonial garments. Only high-ranking officials were allowed to care for them. One white elephant was pampered with meals equal to the king's food, but it died from indigestion since elephants need diets quite different from humans to stay healthy.

In 1854, a white elephant was delivered to King Mongkut. People lined the banks of the Chao Phraya River to welcome the elephant and its entourage as they arrived on magnificently carved barges, powered by hundreds of oarsmen. In the center of the procession was a beautiful raft decorated with flowers. Beneath the raft's gorgeous canopy rode the white elephant.

King Mongkut, noblemen, soldiers, musicians, members of the royal family, and servants formed a procession to the river to welcome the elephant. With drums beating and music playing, the elephant was brought ashore and led to a pavilion where Brahman priests conducted a welcoming ceremony.

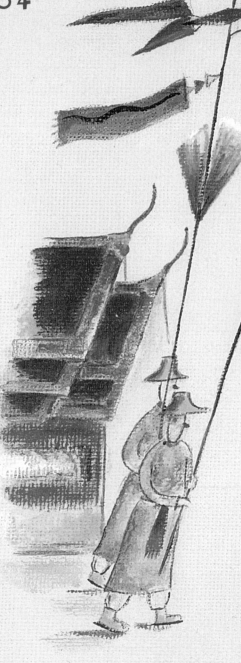

A section of the king's palace became the elephant's home. High-ranking officers, attendants, and slaves cared for his needs. During the elephant's bath, one officer held a crimson-and-gold umbrella while others cooled the animal with golden fans.

A jeweler designed golden rings for his tusks, a golden neck chain, and a gold crown. He was robed in a purple velvet cloak with scarlet and gold fringe.

Later, at a special ceremony, the white elephant was washed, "baptized," and given the rank of prince. The elephant received a stick of sugarcane, which was probably his favorite part of the whole affair!

Rhino Overthrow: *Cacareco*

COUNTRY: Brazil   YEAR: 1959

It's not easy being a rhinoceros. First you have to worry about finding seventy pounds of food each day. Then you have to put up with oxpecker birds having a picnic on the bugs digging into your hide. If that's not enough, you also have to worry about extinction.

No one knows for sure whether four-and-a-half-year-old Cacareco, a 2,400-pound rhinoceros, was worried about anything on October 7, 1959. She wasn't especially pretty, except to rhinoceros lovers. Even her name means "rubbish" or "weakling." But Cacareco was destined for greatness. She was a black African rhino (*Diceros bicornis*) living in Brazil's Rio de Janeiro zoo.

In 1959 Cacareco was loaned to the new São Paulo zoo to celebrate its grand opening. Outside the zoo that year, trouble was brewing. The 3.5 million citizens of São Paulo, Brazil's largest city, were angry about food shortages, the high cost of living, unpaved streets, and open sewers. The voters, who blamed the city council, were ready to protest.

There were forty-five vacant city council seats and 540 candidates running for the offices. But many voters thought the rhinoceros was more qualified than the humans. More than one hundred thousand people wrote in the rhino's name on their ballots, and the rhinoceros won in a landslide victory!

Cacareco got fifteen percent of the votes, which was more than any of the 540 candidates. At the time, it was the highest total for a local candidate in Brazil's history. The closest runner-up (a human) received only 10,079 votes.

Thirteen years later, Cacareco's victory was memorialized when a Canadian political party was named the Rhinoceros Party. The "Rhinos" formed as a lampoon—a kind of joke. Their platform included repealing the law of gravity and giving tax credits to Canadians for sleeping!

Monkey Business: *Taio*

COUNTRY: Brazil   **YEAR:** 1988

Taio was probably the shortest candidate who ever ran for office in Rio de Janeiro. He might also have been the hairiest.

Taio was a chimpanzee at the Rio City Zoo, and in 1988 he was the Banana Party's candidate for mayor. The party's campaign slogan was Vote Monkey—Get Monkey!

If Taio got annoyed, he boldly spit at zoo visitors or threw dirt and sand. Occasionally he would even fling feces (uh . . . doo-doo) at anyone who displeased him. Although he engaged in "dirty politics," he was a leading mayoral candidate and came in third with more than four hundred thousand votes.

When Taio died eight years later in December 1996, flags at the zoo were lowered to half-mast; Mayor Cesar Maia (a human) said that Taio "demonstrated the joyfulness of Rio." The chimp was almost thirty-four years old, which is equivalent to about eighty in human years.

NORTH AMERICA

Gone to the Dogs: *Bosco*

COUNTRY: United States—California   **YEAR:** 1980

Was it just a joke? Maybe. But joke or not, Bosco the dog was elected mayor of Sunol, California, in 1980. Wearing a red bow tie, the black Labrador beat two human candidates.

Sunol is an unincorporated town, a place too small to have its own city government. It is actually governed by elected county supervisors—humans. So Bosco didn't have a lot of responsibilities.

But as a dog-mayor, Bosco received worldwide attention in 1990 when Chinese newspapers ridiculed American democracy and accused the United States government of "going to the dogs."

Perhaps.

But Bosco was loyal and friendly, and he never lied. He served in the position until 1991, when his family moved to a nearby town and he was forced into retirement.

Pussyfooting Around: *Paisley and Company*

COUNTRY: United States—Colorado
YEARS: 1988, 1990, 1991, 1993

Guffey is a small town in Colorado's Rocky Mountains. In 1988, a lovely lady named Paisley was elected mayor. But Paisley wasn't a person. She was a calico cat.

Statistics indicate cats spend eighty percent of their time sleeping. It's hard to imagine how a cat could squeeze holding a political office into such a busy schedule. But Paisley did a terrific job and served three years until her death in 1990.

Since Paisley had been such an outstanding mayor, the town elected another cat to fill the vacant position. Smudge le Plume, described as "mostly Siamese," served until she went missing in October 1991.

By this time, the town residents were so pleased with their feline politicians that they drafted another calico cat to be mayor. This cat had no name, so the children of Wink, Texas, held a naming contest. A sixth-grade boy submitted the winning entry, Whiffey la Gone. The residents of Guffey had been trying to get the county to make improvements. When officials finally paved the road through the town and built a community center, residents credited the cat-mayors. Whiffey served until 1993, when she moved to a ranch.

Then the town went to the dogs, and Shanda, a golden retriever, became the town's mayor. Residents found Shanda to be a politician who really listened, although she did not return phone calls. One issue on Shanda's political platform was that she opposed leash laws. Shanda's fame spread worldwide when she was featured on a national television show, *The Oprah Winfrey Show*.

PAISLEY

SMUDGE LE PLUME

WHIFFEY LA GONE

Going Hog Wild: *Pigasus*

COUNTRY: United States—Illinois   **YEAR:** 1968

In 1968, a group of friends were concerned about the future of the United States. They opposed the Vietnam War and planned to protest at the Democratic National Convention in August.

While the Democratic Convention nominated a presidential candidate, the group, which later became known as the Chicago Seven, planned to nominate its own candidate: a pig! The possibilities seemed endless: pig campaign buttons, pig bumper stickers, pig campaign offices. And after the pig was elected, there would be an in-hoguration.

The group drove out into the Illinois countryside and paid a pig farmer twenty-five dollars for a six-month-old pig who weighed two hundred pounds. They named him Pigasus. Pigasus had lived a normal pig life up until that day, which meant he was dirty and smelly; and he did not favor a trip to the city in a car.

Despite Pigasus's noisy and unpleasant protests, the Chicago Seven took the pig to Chicago's Civic Center for a nominating ceremony. Oddly, the police thought the group was disrupting the peace and arrested them. Pigasus never even made it to a bumper sticker. While the group was being held at the police station, one of the officers said, "Gentlemen, I have some bad news. The pig squealed!"

Getting His Goat: *Clay Henry*

COUNTRY: United States—Texas   YEAR: 1986

Goat Mountain is in southwestern Texas. Not surprisingly, the town of Lajitas, Texas, less than sixty-five miles away, elected a goat as mayor. It happened this way: In 1986, the citizens of Lajitas were voting for a mayor. The candidates were an unusual mix: a man who lived in Houston, which is about five hundred miles away; a wooden statue of a Native American that stood outside the local trading post; a local dog named Buster; and a goat named Clay Henry.

The goat won in a landslide, although no one is certain of the vote count. That's just the way it is in this small town of less than one hundred residents.

Clay Henry served as mayor until his death in 1992, at the age of twenty-three. The next mayor was another goat—Clay Henry, Jr. He left office in 1998, and Clay Henry III took over the job. Since not many towns have goats as their mayors, each Clay Henry mayor has been a popular tourist attraction. Visitors can see the mayor in his pen next to the trading post.

The goat-mayors share an unusual talent: Each one has learned to drink out of a beverage bottle. Tourists buy a bottled beverage and offer it to the goat. Clay Henry takes the bottle in his mouth, guzzles till it is empty, and tosses the empty bottle on the ground.

Mule Rule: *Boston Curtis*

COUNTRY: United States—Washington State   **YEAR:** 1936

Who was Boston Curtis?

Maybe that's the question the voters should have asked.

In 1936, Ken Simmons, the mayor of Milton, Washington, took a mule named Boston Curtis to the county courthouse. Simmons paid the filing fee and, on the filing papers, used the animal's hoofprint in place of a fingerprint. With that, Boston Curtis was registered to run in the primary election.

Boston Curtis never made a campaign promise. He never made a speech. He never even made an appearance, so no one noticed he was a mule.

Evidently no one asked who Boston Curtis was, as the mule was elected to the post of committeeman. Boston Curtis won the election in a landslide victory—52 to 0! And the election went down in history as "the donkey incident." Strange, since everyone knows that a mule is not a donkey.

BIBLIOGRAPHY

Dogs Rule: Ethiopia's Dog-King

Budge, Sir E. A. Wallis, Kt. *A History of Ethiopia.* Vol. 1. Oosterhout N. B., The Netherlands: Anthropological Publications, 1966.

Dale-Green, Patricia. *Lore of the Dog.* Boston: Houghton Mifflin, 1967.

Rackham, H. *Pliny—Natural History*, Volume II, Libri III–VII. Cambridge, MA: Harvard University Press, 1938.

Trew, Cecil G. *The Story of the Dog and His Uses to Mankind.* London: Methuen & Co., Ltd., 1940.

Horse Sense: Incitatus

Barrett, Anthony A. *Caligula: The Corruption of Power.* New Haven, CT: Yale University Press, 1989.

Bryant, Mark. *Casanova's Parrot and Other Tales of the Famous and Their Pets.* New York: Carroll & Graf, 2002.

———. *Private Lives: Curious Facts About the Famous and Infamous.* London: Cassell & Co., 2001.

Tremain, Ruthven. *The Animals' Who's Who.* New York: Charles Scribner's Sons, 1982.

You Dirty Dog: King Henry I's Dog

Barloy, J. J. *Man and Animals: 100 Centuries of Friendship.* London and New York: Gordon & Cremonesi, 1974.

Contamine, Philippe. *War in the Middle Ages.* Translated by Michael Jones. New York: Blackwell Publishers, 1984.

Mery, Fernand. *The Life, History and Magic of the Dog.* New York: Grosset & Dunlap, 1968.

Sisa, Stephen. *The Spirit of Hungary.* Toronto: Rákóczi Foundation, Inc., 1983.

Stubbs, William. *Germany in the Early Middle Ages: 476–1250.* New York: Howard Fertig, 1969.

Tremain, Ruthven. *Animals' Who's Who.* New York: Charles Scribner's Sons, 1982.

It's a Dog's Life: King Saur

Barloy, J. J. *Man and Animals: 10 Centuries of Friendship.* London and New York: Gordon & Cremonesi, 1974.

Coren, Stanley. *The Intelligence of Dogs: A Guide to the Thoughts, Emotions, and Inner Lives of Our Canine Companions.* New York: Bantam Books, 1994.

Dale-Green, Patricia. *Lore of the Dog.* Boston: Houghton Mifflin, 1967.

Hausman, Gerald, and Loretta Hausman. *The Mythology of Dogs: Canine Legend and Lore Through the Ages.* New York: St. Martin's Press, 1997.

Leach, Maria. *God Had a Dog: Folklore of the Dog.* New Brunswick, NJ: Rutgers University Press, 1961.

Sturluson, Snorri. *Heimskringla.* [*The Stories of the Kings of Norway—Called the Round of the World.* Vol. I, II, IV. Translated by William Morris and Eirikr Magnusson.] London: Bernard Quaritch, 1893, 1894, 1905.

Trew, Cecil G. *The Story of the Dog and His Uses to Mankind.* London: Methuen & Co., Ltd., 1940.

Puppy Love: Emperor Ling Ti's Pekingese Dogs

Collier, V. W. F. *Dogs of China and Japan in Nature and Art.* New York: Frederick A. Stokes Company Publishers, 1921.

Coren, Stanley. *The Pawprints of History: Dogs and the Course of Human Events.* New York: The Free Press, 2002.

Dale-Green, Patricia. *Lore of the Dog.* Boston: Houghton Mifflin, 1967.

Godden, Rumer. *The Butterfly Lions: The Story of the Pekingese in History, Legend, and Art.* New York: The Viking Press, 1977.

Thurston, Mary Elizabeth. *The Lost History of the Canine Race: Our 15,000-Year Love Affair with Dogs.* Kansas City, MO: Andrews and McMeel, 1996.

The Cat's Meow: Myobu No Omoto

Hamilton, Elizabeth. *Cats, a Celebration.* New York: Charles Scribner's Sons, 1979.

Kohen, Elli. *World History and Myths of Cats.* Lewiston, NY: The Edwin Mellen Press, 2003.

Morris, Desmond. *Cat World: A Feline Encyclopedia.* New York: Penguin Group, 1996.

Tremain, Ruthven. *Animals' Who's Who.* New York: Charles Scribner's Sons, 1982.

Day of the Jackal: A Hero of India

Haq, S. Moinul. *Khafi Khan's History of Alamgir.* Kakachi-5: Pakistan Historical Society, 1975.

Hawkridge, Emma. *Indian Gods and Kings: The Story of a Living Past.* Boston: Houghton Mifflin, 1935.

Jackson, A. V. Williams, ed. *History of India.* Vol. IV. London: The Grolier Society Publishers, 1903, 1906.

Sarkar, Sir Jadunath. *Short History of Aurangzib: 1618–1707.* Calcutta: M. C. Sarkar & Sons Private Ltd., 1962.

White Elephant: The Elephants of the Siamese Court

Carrington, Richard. *Elephants: A Short Account of Their Natural History, Evolution and Influence on Mankind.* New York: Basic Books, Inc., 1959.

Delort, Robert. *The Life and Lore of the Elephant.* New York: Harry N. Abrams, Inc., Publishers, 1992.

Eltringham, S. K. *Elephants.* Poole, Dorset, U.K.: Blandford Books, Ltd., 1982.

Ringis, Rita. *Elephants of Thailand in Myth, Art, and Reality.* Oxford, U.K.: Oxford University Press, 1996.

Walsh, William. *Curiosities of Popular Customs and of Rites, Ceremonies, Observances, and Miscellaneous Antiquities.* Philadelphia and London: J. B. Lippincott Co., 1925.

Rhino Overthrow: Cacareco

Brooks, Stephen. *Canadian Democracy: An Introduction.* 3rd ed. Toronto: Oxford University Press, 2000.

Colombo, John Roberts. *Colombo's Canadian References.* Toronto: Oxford University Press, 1976.

De Carvalho, George. "Rhino Horns in on a Brazilian Election." *Life,* October 19, 1959, 54.

Dulles, John W. *Unrest in Brazil: Political-Military Crises 1955–1964.* Austin: University of Texas Press, 1970.

"Hemisphere. Brazil: The Rhino Vote." *Time,* October 19, 1959, 46.

New York Times, "Rhino Takes Brazilian Election Victory with Aplomb." October 9, 1959.

"Rhino's Victory." *Senior Scholastic* 75 (October 21, 1959): 21.

Szulc, Tad. "Rhinoceros Elected in Brazilian Protest." *New York Times,* October 8, 1959.

Tremain, Ruthven. *Animals' Who's Who.* New York: Charles Scribner's Sons, 1982.

Wallace, Bruce. "The Rhinos Are Coming." *Maclean's* 97 (September 3, 1984): 23.

Monkey Business: Tiao

Astor, Michael. "Zoo Vote in Brazil Pits Chimps off the Old Block." *Houston Chronicle,* August 17, 1997, 4-star edition, news sec. A.

Bloom, Roger. "Death Is Good Indicator of Country's Uniqueness." *The Florida Times-Union,* March 30, 1997, City edition, travel sec. http://infoweb.newsbank.com/.

Kohut, John J., and Roland Sweet. *Strange Tails: All-too-True News from the Animal Kingdom.* New York: Plume, 1999.

"Rio Mourns Death of Beloved Chimp." *Buffalo News,* December 26, 1996, City edition, news sec. http://infoweb.newsbank.com/.

"Rio Mourns Political Chimp." *Washington Times,* December 25, 1996, 2nd edition, world sec. http://infoweb.newsbank.com/.

Gone to the Dogs: Bosco

Kristof, Nicholas D. "Chinese Press Harps on 'Dark Side' of U.S. Life." *San Francisco Chronicle,* April 12, 1990.

"Residents Doggedly Pound Bushes in Search for Mayor." *Arizona Republic,* November 27, 1987.

Stephens, John Richard. *Weird History 101.* Holbrook, MA: Adams Media Corp., 1997.

Pussyfooting Around: Paisley and Company

Altman, Roberta. *The Quintessential Cat: A Connoisseur's Guide to the Cat in History, Art, Literature, and Legend.* New York: Macmillan, 1994.

Garner, Joe. "Town Puts Cat in Catbird Seat." *Rocky Mountain News,* March 2, 1988.

Jones, Rebecca. "The 10 Best Animal Stories from Talking Pigs to Frozen Caimans; Here's *The News*'s Pick of the Litter." *Rocky Mountain News,* June 2, 1989.

Krakel, Dean. "Taking Cat out of the Bag Put Town on the Map." *Rocky Mountain News,* October 28, 1991.

Nash, Bruce, and Allan Zullo. *Amazing but True Cat Tales.* Kansas City, MO: Andrews McMeel, 1993.

O'Driscoll, Patrick. "'Demo-cat' Pussyfoots into Office; Smudge le Plume, Feline Chief of Guffy, Called 'A Great Politician.'" *Denver Post,* April 7, 1991.

"Town's Mayor Missing; Some Fear Fowl Play." *Washington Times,* October 29, 1991.

Going Hog Wild: Pigasus

Raskin, Jonah. *For the Hell of It: The Life and Times of Abbie Hoffman.* Berkeley: University of California Press, 1996.

Rath, Sara. *The Complete Pig: An Entertaining History of Pigs.* Stillwater, MN: Voyageur Press, 2000.

Rubin, Jerry. "Inside the Great Pigasus Plot." *Ramparts* 8 (December 1969): 11–14.

Sloman, Larry. *Steal This Dream: Abbie Hoffman and the Countercultural Revolution in America.* New York: Doubleday, 1998.

Whitfield, Stephen J. "The Stuntman: Abbie Hoffman 1936–1989." *The Virginia Quarterly Review* 66, no. 4 (Autumn 1990): 568–569.

Getting His Goat: Clay Henry

Lajitas, The Ultimate Hideout. "About Us: Mayor Clay Henry III." http://www.lajitas.com/mayor.html.

"The Six-Pack Kid." *Time,* September 6, 1982, 25.

The Year of the Goat. "Clay Henry III, Goat Mayor of Lajitas." http://www.karlschatz.com/yearofthegoat/archives/000089.shtml (February 2, 2004).

Mule Rule: Boston Curtis

Elwood, Ann, and Carol Orsag Madigan. *The Macmillan Book of Fascinating Facts: An Almanac for Kids.* New York: Macmillan, 1989.

Heritage League of Pierce County. *A History of Pierce County Washington.* Portland, OR: 1990.

Obituaries of Boston Curtis. *Tacoma News Tribune,* December 30, 1981.

INDEX